Dream a
dream, then
make a
plan — the "magic"
is in your hands.
Jackie Kelly

4/2023
To Lucca,
Hope you love
this story as much
as I do!
we do!
Love,
Grammy xoxo
& Papa

Roxie's
Fairy Adventure
at
THE PEABODY

Dedication

from the author, Jackie Kelly

For Sophie, Lucy, Vera and Gwen … may your lives
always be filled will magical moments.

And for fairy lovers everywhere … including two lovely
little ones, Brianna Belz Fargotstein and Harper Hubbard.

Special thanks to:
My husband Fred for his unfailing faith in me …
along with Fred, Lizzie, Jonathan, Val, Sophie, Lucy, Vera and
Gwen—the best family anyone could ever have.

And to:
Greg Belz in memory of his best friend, Bentley.

Dedication

from the illustrator, Morgan Spicer

To my sister Samantha and her wee little lady,
Eliana Drew. I cannot wait to read this with you both.

To my Grandma D, I am forever grateful for your
support of my work and where it's helped me go.

To my Nanny and Grandmama, who I miss very much.

Now you may think you know all about fairies. You probably know there are colorful flower fairies and shy woods fairies, but did you know there are river fairies? Well, there are.

These fairies live in very tall trees near lovely, big rivers.

They're brave and loyal
and VERY adventurous.

One of these fairies
is named Roxie.

She lives beside the
Mississippi River in Memphis,
Tennessee, and this is the story
of one of her biggest adventures.

"Today's the day!"
Roxie exclaimed as she
hopped out of her cozy
little bed one morning.

She flew to her bedroom window high in the hollow oak tree and looked out at the river boats going under the Mississippi River Bridge.

"The kind of day when dreams come true!"

Roxie's dream involved the grandest hotel in the city,

The Peabody Memphis.

She could see it from her house in the tall tree.

The Peabody Memphis stretched high up into the air and had a beautiful rooftop terrace overlooking the river. Roxie had flown all the way up to the lighted sign on the very top of the hotel—in fact that's how she had met Colonel Bart—

but she had never,

ever

been inside the grand hotel itself.

Colonel Bart was a mallard duck—the most distinguished-looking
mallard duck Roxie had ever seen.

She first met him on the rooftop of The Peabody at the
Duck Palace that the Peabody ducks called home.
These lucky ducks spent their nights in the Duck Palace
and their days swimming in the glamorous Peabody fountain
right in the middle of the enormous Peabody lobby.

Colonel Bart told her all about the lives of the Peabody ducks, and that made her want to see the inside of the Peabody more than ever. "Every morning the Duckmaster comes up to the Duck Palace," Colonel Bart told her, "'It's show time!' he'll say … and then all 5 of us ducks march into the Peabody elevator for the trip down to the lobby."

Sometimes, Roxie couldn't help interrupting, "And when the doors open, marching music begins to play—and you all march out onto an honest-to-goodness red carpet—the kind they use for movie stars," and then Roxie would flutter her wings until she rose up a couple of feet into the air.

"And people crowd around us and take pictures," the Colonel would continue, "but we keep marching—right up to the magnificent fountain right in the center of the lobby."

"Then you swim in that fountain ... all ... day ... long," Roxie would sigh. "I wish I could see the Peabody lobby," she said, but she knew she couldn't.

Fairies were NOT allowed to be seen by humans … and the Peabody lobby is always full of humans. But one day Colonel Bart thought of a very clever plan to help Roxie's dream come true, and today, he and Roxie were going to put that plan into action!

Roxie flew out of her tree house as fast as her wings would take her — straight to the Duck Palace.

It wasn't long before the Duckmaster arrived, announcing 'It's show time!' And the ducks lined up and stepped into the Peabody elevator. The elevator door closed behind them.

But Roxie
was nowhere
to be seen.

The elevator doors opened into the grand lobby, and out came the Duckmaster in his top hat and red jacket, followed by the Peabody ducks: Patricia, Kiara, Phoebe, Penelope, and the Colonel—but still no Roxie.

The ducks marched down the red carpet and hopped into the fountain with Patricia leading the way. The crowd took lots of pictures, and gave them a round of applause. Where could Roxie be?

Everyone was watching the Peabody ducks, but nobody watched quite as hard as two young sisters named Sophie and Lucy and their little cousin, Vera.

Lucy was looking SO hard that she saw two little eyes peering out from behind Kiara's wing.

"Look, Sophie! A fairy!"

"Don't be silly, Lucy," said big sister Sophie. "Even though fairies really ARE real, everyone knows that WE aren't allowed to see them." She paused and looked harder.

Could that be a fairy wing?

"Look, Mom!" Lucy tugged at her mom's sleeve.

But their mom didn't hear her. In fact, nobody heard her except Roxie.

Vera pointed at Kiara. "Wing?"

"Oh, no!" Roxie thought. "That human SAW me! I have to convince her she didn't see a fairy at all!"

"Psssst!" she hissed as Patricia swam by. "Patricia! Help! Make everyone look at you while I find a place to hide!"

Patricia sprang into action. She quacked loudly and flapped her wings. Then she hopped right out of the fountain and onto the floor where all the people were standing. As they scurried out of Patricia's way, Roxie flew straight up into the elegant chandelier.

"Whew! That was close," she said as the Duckmaster herded Patricia back into the fountain. "But wow! This place is fabulous—even more beautiful than the Colonel said." She looked down at the fountain below, the magnificent carpet, and the enormous grand piano that could play a tune all by itself.

Then she re-directed her gaze to the crowd of humans. Sophie and Lucy were looking all around, and eventually their eyes moved upward toward the chandelier.

Roxie zoomed down to hide behind a potted plant on a table below and looked around. Nobody saw a thing! But Lucy and Sophie were still looking. They looked high. They looked low.

"I KNOW I saw a fairy, Mommy!" Lucy said.

"Well, maybe you were wrong," said big sister Sophie.

Mom just smiled. "We need to catch up with Vera and her mom."

"And baby Gwen!" Sophie chimed in.

"Ready to go to the gift shop?" Mom asked

"Yessssssss!" said the sisters. And off they went.

For the rest of the day Roxie enjoyed the wonderful sights and sounds of the grand old hotel. She watched the humans from a hiding place in the chandelier. She bumped along on the inside of the player piano as it played its tunes. She hid in the potted plants.

That afternoon when the ducks marched back into the elevator, the Colonel felt the tickle of fairy wings behind his right wing.

"Thank you, Colonel," Roxie whispered, "for making my dreams come true. The Peabody is truly the most wonderful place ever!"

And then Patricia, Kiara, Phoebe, Penelope and the Colonel—
and Roxie—rode the elevator back to the Duck Palace on the
roof of the grand hotel.

But that's not the end of the story.

No, indeed. It's really only the beginning. Because Roxie loved The Peabody Hotel so much, she comes back whenever she can.

So, when you visit The Peabody Memphis, be sure to look around the beautiful, grand lobby. Watch the Peabody ducks as they swim in the fountain. Listen to the wonderful old grand piano that can play music all by itself.

But most of all, keep an eye out for Roxie. She doesn't want you to see her, because you ARE a human after all, but if you look for her really hard in all her hiding places, well, maybe— just maybe—you'll catch a glimpse of her, too…just like Sophie and Lucy did.

The End.

About the Author

Jackie has believed in the magic of fairies—and the magic of the world-famous Peabody Hotel—since childhood. So, perhaps she was destined to tell the story of an adventurous river fairy who dreams of exploring the grand old hotel—despite the fact that fairies AREN'T allowed to be seen by humans.

"I've written for radio, TV, print, and corporate clients, and I've enjoyed it all, but nothing has given me quite as much pleasure as writing about Roxie, the fairy who enlists the Peabody ducks to help her dream come true. I dedicate this book to my four young granddaughters— who know a thing or two about fairy stories themselves—with the hope that they'll remember that creativity, like love, lasts a lifetime."

—Jackie Kelly

About the Illustrator

Morgan Spicer is the founder of Bark Point Studio. She is also an illustrator, character designer, animal advocate, ethical vegan, TV/film addict and the proud parent of three rescue dogs. Morgan Spicer has illustrated 16 books while also creating custom animal art for her Bark Point Studio subscribers. A percentage of many of these works are donated to animal rescues and shelters across the country. It is her ultimate dream to open an animal rescue, sanctuary and studio (Bark Pointé) to continue educating youth about the magic, friendship and responsibility that comes with animal companionship.